THE PLEASURE OF DROWNING

JEAN BÜRLESK

WINNER OF THE
PRIX D'ENCOURAGEMENT
DE LA FONDATION SERVAIS 2019

Luna Press
PUBLISHING

Text Copyright © 2020 Jean Bürlesk
Cover Design © 2020 Carolina Cancanilla

First published by Luna Press Publishing, Edinburgh, 2020

The right of Jean Bürlesk to be identified as the Author of the Work has been asserted by her in accordance with the Copyright, Designs and Patents Act 1988.

The Pleasure of Drowning © 2020. All rights reserved. No part of this book may be used or reproduced in any manner for the purpose of training artificial intelligence technologies or systems. No part of this publication may be reproduced, stored in a retrieval system, or transmitted in any form or by any means, electronic, mechanical, photocopy, recording or otherwise, without prior written permission of the copyright owners. Nor can it be circulated in any form of binding or cover other than that in which it is published and without similar condition including this condition being imposed on a subsequent purchaser.

The views and opinions expressed in this book are those of the author and do not necessarily reflect the opinions or beliefs of the publisher and its affiliates.

www.lunapresspublishing.com

ISBN-13: 978-1-913387-20-4

TO MARGUERITE THOMAS-CLEMENT
AND ALL THE PEOPLE WHO INSPIRE

CONTENTS

YESTERDAY UPON THE STAIR
I MET A MAN WHO WASN'T THERE
HE WASN'T THERE AGAIN TODAY
I WISH, I WISH HE'D GO AWAY

- HUGHES MEARNS, ANTIGONISH (1899)

HAIR

My hair is an act of faith.

So Mother told me.

I didn't have much hair, as a child. What little hair I did have was thin and brown and brittle. And soon enough, that was gone as well. Mother is a woman of wisdom and power, but even she couldn't find a remedy to my early calvity. As time passed and my skull stayed bare, Mother grew ever more desperate. She grew so desperate in fact, that, having long since exhausted her list of potions and poultices, and despite her singular lack of dogmatic inclination, she finally turned to a more unlikely source of help: she took to praying.

She prayed to every god and every spirit she could find and, when none of it yielded the desired result, she started praying to the Lord himself. She made a vow to him, a vow so secret and so terrible, she never revealed its content to anyone, not even me. If only I could grow hair, she promised …

Whatever it was she had promised, it must have been deemed an acceptable sacrifice. The fact being that, when Mother performed her daily inspection of my skull the next morn, she thought she felt a light stubble under her fingers, not quite enough to be certain, not yet, but enough to send her heart fluttering in a frenzy.

By the second day, there was no longer room for any doubt: my hair was growing, and it was growing strong and dense and fair. Mother threw a feast that Sunday, and invited anyone who would come. A dozen villages were represented at this *my hair-day*, and I was given apples and nuts and honey and pies and – best of all – ribbons for my new-grown hair.

That was ten years ago, and my hair hasn't stopped growing since. I have the longest and most beautiful hair in all the land and my suitors are so numerous that Mother had me locked up in a tower. I do not mind much, for the hair takes up all my time anyway, as I need several hours to brush it every day – too much time for me to wish to go out and let the wind destroy all my hard work. Nor do I like to move around too much, for the hair weighs me down and makes my every movement slow. The tower is as good a place as any and far more spacious than Mother's house, spacious enough to accommodate the growth of my hair for months to come.

I do worry, though.

I worry my hair might grow so heavy my neck will snap under the strain. I worry my hair might grow so dense I shall no longer be able to part it and look at the sun. I worry my hair might grow so wild it will strangle me in my sleep. I tried cutting it, but it grew back. I tried tearing it out, but the roots burrowed deep into my skull. The Lord only knows what my hair is going to do next. But I'm scared.

AFTERWORD

You've made it.

You've reached the afterword. And so little has changed since you were looking at the cover. See, books aren't dangerous. Except, of course, when you read them. Or use them to hit someone over the head.

Okay, so this one's got a creepy title. But, let's be honest, that's at least part of the reason you opened it. I'll have to disappoint you, though: I have never taken pleasure in drowning anyone. Nor have I ever taken pleasure in being drowned.[1] I have, however, experienced the feeling of drowning and revelled in it. Water doesn't come into it.

The characters in this book don't drown in water. They drown in love, in life, in lies. One of them drowns in wine. Or in blood. Or in blood that is wine. It's all a matter of perspective. Anyway – they drown in many

---

1. Incidentally, I have never drowned anyone or been drowned myself.

things, ranging from their own physical or metaphysical being to the concept of narrative. They don't all survive their drowning, but many do. Sometimes it changes them. Sometimes it doesn't.

My hope is you will drown as well, if just for a moment. That's the whole point of this book.[2] Don't worry, though. I won't claim drowning in words is one of the less dangerous ways of drowning, but I hereby do affirm it is one of the most pleasurable ones.

[Editor's Note: We tried getting the author to include some useful information here, but he wouldn't budge. Instead, you might want to check out the foreword for context on the stories and further titbits. It's at the back. Yes, we know. He wouldn't budge on that either.]

---

2. That, and to make me rich and famous. But not too rich, and not too famous. Just the right amount of rich and famous … Not bloody likely? Oh well.

FOUNDATIONS

She was waiting for him.

She knew he'd be back.

She loved listening to his voice: so excited, so exciting, so wild and wilful and reliably unreliable. It would escape his grasp from time to time, becoming thin, strained or breaking. He always took a deeper tone after that, as if trying to reassert his masculinity. Silly boy. Wonderfully silly boy. So passionate, so thoughtful, so witty and intelligent. What language would he be using today? Would it be French, German, English, Spanish? Maybe even Luxembourgish? She loved that language, silly little language, a private joke stubbornly maintaining itself amongst the larger beasts. She loved so many things about this place … Whatever the language, he would be here, he had said as much. How grateful she had been to the Spaniard for asking. Oh, let him use Luxembourgish today – his home tongue, the language of his heart, as he would say, though he did have a slight accent when he used it. It made her think of her late husband, strange as that might seem – he had spoken nothing of the sort. But it was the language of the Luxembourgers, that it was, and out of some strange fancy they called her husband the first Luxembourger; it would have made him laugh to hear it, with his wonderfully deep, sad laugh. Oh, how she missed that laugh!

There it was again. Barely realising it, she had done it again. All her hard work. Was it the young man? Was he the reason? Or was it the memory of her husband? Did she not want to see his legacy … She loved him still, after all this time. Despite it all. Despite his betrayal. She really loved that bloody fool … Maybe it wasn't him. Maybe it wasn't either of them. Maybe it was the place itself. She had grown quite fond of it over the years. She had hated it at first, obviously. She had raged against the narrow walls, against the unfairness of it all … Still, it would be quite a pity. But what was the point of weaving the damn shroud if she always ended up undoing her own work?

But there *he* was, that was *his* voice and at first she didn't know the words, so excited was she to have him back. It wasn't French or Spanish, that it wasn't, nor was it Portuguese, Italian, Romanian, Latin, … No, it was a Germanic language, sure enough, though it wasn't Luxembourgish, that ridiculous-joke-of-a-silly-little-language, wonderfully silly language that didn't have a verb for loving, but used a protracted construction, something like 'I hold you dear' – at least that was what he would claim, but of course he was lying, it didn't have the poetry, though it did have the emotion, so much emotion, ech-hunn-dech-gär … 'I have you fondly'; truly, that's what it meant: 'I have you fondly'. Silly little language, making things so complicated and rightly so, rightly so; love wasn't easy, why should saying it be? Her husband had never told her he loved her, but he had, he had, and it had driven him mad. No, it wasn't Luxembourgish, and it wasn't German, but it was … what? It couldn't … it couldn't be Dutch, could it? There were always so many people speaking Dutch when summer came – and there had been for a while, a ridiculously short, agonisingly long while … But he didn't speak Dutch, did he? He certainly didn't, and the language, she realised in a short outburst of laughter, the language he spoke today was English, and a funny language that was, too.

"Welcome to the Bock promontory," he intoned, dramatically, "the cradle of the city (*Welcome*, she thought to herself, excitedly. *Welcome*) – it's the location of the first castle and it remains a central position at the time of the fortress (*Castle*, she thought. *Fortress*). Now, we've mentioned the four plateaus of the city: the central plateau behind you, the Kirchberg on your left, the Rahm and the plateau Bourbon on your right, separated by the valleys of the Pétrusse and the Alzette … (*Pétrusse. Alzette*). The importance of the Bock promontory comes from its position at the centre of it all. That's why Siegfried built his castle here, overlooking the entire valley and the two Roman roads that crossed one another at this place (*Oh, Siegfried*, she thought). It's also why the Bock promontory and the Bock casemates underneath it were home to a battery of fifty cannons at the time of the fortress.   Fifty-cannons-and-up-to-one-thousand-two-hundred-soldiers-ready-to-shoot-into-the-valley-below-or-into-the-outside-forts-on-the-neighbouring-plateaus-if-an-attacker-should-take-one-of-them-by-storm   (She silently applauded)!

"However," he said, and her heart suddenly started beating faster, "however, what we really need to talk about in this place – is this well right here! This, ladies and gentlemen, this is the most important place in the entire city (*Yes, darling*, she felt like shouting. *Yes, it is!*). Now obviously, water is quite important, for the castle, for the fortress, the casemates … but that's not what I'm talking about. The fortress had a total of six wells. This one is important for a different reason … Remember how Siegfried built his first castle here for military, strategic, economic and political reasons (*Boring! Get to the story, darling, get to the story*)? Well, you can forget all of that. The real reason Siegfried build his Lucilinburhuc here is because he was walking through the valley one day – when he heard the most beautiful voice rising from the rocks ahead. Entranced, he followed the voice to its source, and what he saw then was nothing less than the most beautiful woman he could ever have imagined (*Most beauuutiful woman!*). He fell in love immediately, but couldn't quite muster the courage to call out to her. When he finally decided to move towards her, a fallen twig cracked under his foot and the woman, startled by the noise, disappeared amongst the bushes (She was so enthralled by his tale – her tale – that she forgot to laugh at the entirely fictional scene). Desperate at the idea he might have missed his only chance, Siegfried moved emperor and bishops in his efforts to acquire the valley. He established himself on the Bock, built his first castle here, his Lucilinburhuc, and spent months searching the valley for his one true love (*He did*, she cried out in jubilation. *He really did!* [Editor's Note: He really didn't]). He did find her eventually," the guide continued. "The woman the young count had fallen for was named Melusina, and she became his wife, she agreed to marry him," he said, and she shuddered, "under one condition.

"One day a week, Melusina would disappear, and Siegfried wasn't allowed to ask any questions. He wasn't allowed to follow her or otherwise enquire about her whereabouts or whatabouts … that day belonged to her alone." The guide paused here for a moment, before adding, as he always did, "Actually kind of practical, isn't it?", earning laughter and applause from the female side of his audience (*Don't make them laugh, my love. It's no laughing matter; you should know that*). "Siegfried accepted, of course, mad with love as he was, and for a while the couple lived quite happily, had several children – the later counts of the city – until, one day, Siegfried simply couldn't do it anymore (Suddenly she wasn't so sure she wanted to hear the story again. Hadn't she earned the right to a reprieve, always playing his most attentive listener?). Driven by curiosity, perhaps suspicion, he followed his wife, and watched as she disappeared into the bathroom. Unable to restrain himself, he knelt to peer through the keyhole … The first thing he glimpsed was the movement of her hair, the glint of the sun reflecting from her golden curls, their strands now interwoven with precious silver. Then he caught sight of her face, the lines on her forehead and her cheeks now deeper and more pronounced, as if time had been wielding a chisel, removing the outer layers to slowly reveal her inner strength and character. Age had not only not diminished her: she was more beautiful than she had ever been. Moved by the beauty of the spectacle, the count suddenly felt shame for his distrust and, in his haste to step away, he stumbled against the door, causing it to swing wide open. Melusina saw her husband standing just a few feet away, she twisted in her bathtub and, where Siegfried expected her legs to appear, scales rose from the water, covering the entire lower half of his wife's body, neatly overlapping in an intricate pattern, her legs gone, her rear end the tail of a fish (His audience let out Oohs and Aahs, but she felt pretty sick just then).

"As Siegfried had broken his word, Melusina was swallowed by the rock. And that, ladies and gentlemen, is the origin of the first well of the city; this well right here!" The tourists broke into exclamations, questions

and laughter of all kind. He ignored them. "But! …
But the story doesn't end there. Apparently, Melusina
is still down there in her well (*You don't need to tell me,*
she thought, darkly). Any of you catch a glimpse of her
yet? No? Oh, you have? (*Not bloody likely. I mean, have
you seen his beer paunch?*) You're not lying to me, sir? (*Of
course he is; you know he is*). Well then, you'd better listen
carefully, because here is what you're going to do.

"Every seven years, Melusina emerges from her well
for one day and finds … some young soldier, perhaps,
at the time of the fortress, or a young tourist, nowadays
… (Laughter. She had heard the joke too many times,
though, plus it made it sound like there had been many
suitors, and that had never been true. Not everyone was
worthy of her affections; she had standards). She has to
find a young man − or a young woman, perhaps, she
might be looking for a young woman … (*Nope. No, she
might not, thank you very much*), what with Siegfried's
faithlessness and now this endless waiting … She might
no longer trust the unfair sex (*Fair point, but still no*).
And remember, she is over a thousand years old (*Thanks
for reminding everyone. That was oh so very thoughtful*).
We are all young in her eyes (*Nope*). So any one of us
could potentially be chosen (*Again: I have standards*).
Though apparently this time around you, sir, are the one
she wants (*Standards!*).

"Once Melusina has shown herself to a person of
her liking, their mission is to present themselves at the

altar of Saint Michael's (*Or Saint Saviour's; we knew it as Saint Saviour's*), the eldest church in the city, at the last strike of midnight, not one moment earlier or later, for ten nights in a row (*And don't you forget it*). Having proven themselves to her in this way, they will, on the tenth night, behold a serpent on the altar, with a key in its mouth. They have to kiss the snake to obtain the key, then go back to the valley and spit it into the river (*Or the well*, she mused. *The well will do just fine. I don't know why they would want to go all the way to the river; it's a detour for me as well*). With that, Melusina will be freed and you, sir, will be free to marry her.

"What do you mean, you already have a wife? You should have thought of that before flirting with Melusina! We fully expect you to marry her once you've saved her from her well (*Like that'll ever happen. He's not the one, sweetheart; you've got to know that*). And save her you shall. I won't take no for an answer (*I will*). Don't worry though, I do believe it's supposed to be a reward, not a punishment; so – despite her thousand years of age – she'll probably still look relatively young and beautiful (She looked at her reflection in the water. There was, she believed, sufficient cause for satisfaction). Anyway, it doesn't matter if she's a derelict old hag (That made her hiss. Now why would he say such a thing?). We really need you to free her, whatever the case, because, and this is really important, if nobody saves Melusina from her well, she has a way of saving herself (*I do. I really do, and I'm getting dangerously close to using it*) ... Every seven years, when she emerges for one day, she also continues working on a gigantic shroud, a shroud that is supposed to cover the entire Bock promontory. If she manages to complete it, she'll go free as well – but the city will fall to ruin." He paused to let the weight of the catastrophe sink in, before adding, in typical British understatement – though British was the last thing he was – "And, well ... that's not my favourite option."

"Surely we can't have that happen. Why don't you try and save Melusina?" asked one of the tourists (*Yes,* she mouthed, regaining her colour. *Oh yes, baby, that's the plan*).

"I would," said he (*You shall,* thought she), "but she hasn't shown herself to me. Apparently, I'm not her type." He laughed (*Well, hellooo. Seven years ago you would still have been half a baby*).

"So, when does she show herself exactly? When do you start counting the seven years?"

"I don't know exactly, I'm afraid. Well, I don't know at all, actually. It would be rather practical to know the date of her next appearance." (*Tomorrow, sweetheart, tomorrow's the day. Just you wait till midnight. A few more hours, and you will look upon my face. A few more hours, and I shall look into your eyes. A-few-more-hours-and-I-will-speak-those-words-you-know-so-well. You shall stand the vigil. You shall kiss the serpent, that lucky thing. You shall bring me the key and I, my love, I shall ... [Editor's*

Note: We had to take out a part of the narration featuring an unseemly display of affection between an amphibian and the wall of a well]).

"So do you do this all year round?"

"Oh no, mostly during summer vacation. Very few people come to visit the city in winter. Plus, I'm not actually here the rest of the time … You're my last tour of the season, as it happens. As soon as we're done here, I'm catching a train. It's back to the toils of academia for me." (Her heart stopped. He wouldn't be here. She could feel herself growing old again). "So, anyway, you know what to do if you see Melusina. The Hollow Tooth might be a fake and, despite the cannon ball in the church tower, there's no reason to believe Münchhausen was ever in Luxembourg, but the one story I ask you not to doubt is the story of Melusina. Our survival depends on it." And, with that, he was gone.

In her dark well, all the darker now for his absence, Melusina prepared for a long day of weaving.

STORIES

OR

NOTHING EVER HAPPENS IN A BAR

You want a story?

What's a story …

A story … is something you tell … something you're told … something you read … something you write …

A story is fiction. A story is words. A story is a lie.

"No great story ever started with someone eating a salad," some idiot once said. Now you can read that on t-shirts … it's all over the *facebook* thing. The idea being that *alcohol* is the best start to a great evening, to a great adventure, to a story worth telling your grandchildren. Yeah, right. What does a great story start with? Damned if I know. It certainly doesn't start in reality. It certainly doesn't start in a bar.

I've seen my fair share of bars, I can tell you. Beer bars … wine bars … Luxembourgish bars … Colombian bars

... English pubs ... French cafés ... sports-bars-biker-bars-college-bars-music-bars-dance-bars-salsa-bars-jazz-bars-comedy-bars ... Mars bars ... sushi bars, salad bars ... gay bars or titty bars ... I've seen bars and bars and bars. Nothing ever happens in a bar.

A bar isn't the place you go to see your life transform into an adventure. It's the place you go to forget that it never will. That's why *I'm* here every fucking day.

So, there you go.

Bars.

Boring.

What I wouldn't give to see something happen for a change ... but it'd be like throwing money into a wishing well. The strangest sight you're likely to find here is silly old me: a creepy man with long hair holding a Mars bar and a soliloquy and *not* telling a story ... Life in a nutshell. Yeaaah, keep looking the other way. Don't let me bother you. Because your life is so much better! Asshole.

Anyone know a story? I could use a good lie right about now ...

I sure used to know some ... ghost stories, those were my favourites. I loved a good ghost story. But how's a ghost story going to scare you when you're half a ghost yourself? I used to have nightmares after a ghost story. I quite miss those nightmares ... But that's the trouble with dreams. You outgrow them.

Look at the girl in the corner, sitting by herself ... Forlorn. That's the word. She looks forlorn. Must be waiting for someone. There used to be a story there. If only I could remember … Come on, it's like you're not even trying! Make an effort, show some good will … Oh, shut up. You're boring me already.

So. Girl in the corner waiting for her long-lost lover out there at sea. Nope. Not a story. Don't want to know. Group of men lost in wine and merriment, celebrating an upcoming wedding or something, with one man at the centre, the one it is all about presumably, pale and livid and oblivious to the world. So not a story. As for you, just looking at you for too long will make me fall asleep. And then there is the crazy guy at the counter, the one without the Mars bar. Hell, I *wish* I was a story.

Lookee there, there's another not-a-story entering the bar. Bit shaken up. Looks like he could use a drink. And, sure enough, he's heading straight for the counter. "What? You're searching for the Holy Grail?" He's searching for the Holy Grail. "Well, who isn't?" He looks relieved.

"Galahad," he tells me. "And you must be Sir Lancelot."

Sure.

Lancelot.

Right.

"You do realise that would make me your father, right? Just saying. And … if I've got to be someone, I'd rather be King Arthur."

He jumps to his feet. Apparently, that was the wrong thing to say. "You're not Lancelot!" he yells.

Geez, I know. No reason to be so upset. I'll get over it.

"Who are you? Are you a spy? Who's your master?" He's reaching for something in his jacket … Is that a gun?

"Look," I say, "calm down. I'm … no one really. I'm not James Bond. Or Lancelot. Nor am I working for anyone. I'm kind of between jobs right now. And I'm unarmed."

That last bit seems to calm him down. "Why would you pretend to be the King?" he asks. Whatever he was reaching for under his jacket he doesn't pull out.

"I wasn't," I assure him. "I wouldn't. I just meant … it would be kind of nice, being King Arthur. Not for the ruling and all that. That sounds like a bore. I don't need the power and the responsibility, the money or the women … The women might be nice. I could go for the women. Anyway, I just meant … he's the one at the centre, you know? He just sits there, sends his knights out on missions, and they come back and tell him stories. I'd love it if there was an army of knights lining up to tell *me* stories."

Galahad ponders this for a while, then agrees that it would, in fact, be nice and – after advising me to stay out of his way – stalks off to sit in the corner opposite the forlorn girl, who now seems to be wistfully contemplating the group of celebrating men. Funny that Galahad should have a gun, though. And kind of absurd, considering he's supposed to be a medieval knight, out on a holy quest or something. It probably wasn't a gun. Why should he have a gun?

I've almost decided that what Galahad is hiding under his jacket couldn't possibly be a gun or, if it is, then surely no more than a water pistol, when another man steps into the bar. He looks around, scrutinising the faces of everyone in the room, and heads towards me (*Why me?* I wonder), then goes for Galahad instead.

In a flash, Galahad jumps to his feet, pulls the water pistol from his jacket and starts firing real bullets at the stranger. Unimpressed, the newcomer draws a lightsabre and uses it to deflect the bullets as they reach him. One of them ricochets and hits the forlorn girl in the shoulder. The wedding party starts shrieking. I grab the nearest stool and prepare to throw it at someone … except none of this is actually happening.

Come on. I mean, with the best will in the world, or at least in the city … whichever city … Luxembourg, probably, or Avalon, if you will … you can't possibly expect me to think you'd believe as ludicrous a story as this.

The man without the lightsabre reaches Galahad's table unimpeded and, while the knight stares into a cup, he starts telling him something in a low but solemn voice. I can't quite make out the words, but they seem to be reverberating throughout the room. It's as if the entire world has fallen silent and nothing matters anymore, save for those words …

My phone is vibrating. Three missed calls. Would you believe it. Oh, and one text. "Will you be home at six o'clock sharp?" It's midnight.

"No," I reply, helpfully.

When I look back up, the man without the lightsabre is nowhere to be seen. Galahad has collapsed on his table, his head resting in a puddle of some dark liquid … I hadn't realised he was already that drunk. Well then. Like I said: nothing ever happens in a bar.

CINDERELLA IN THE SHOE

She couldn't see anything from her room high atop the tower, but she could hear. She would listen to the household and know all the talk of the city. And there was really only one kind of talk in the city: her prince was looking for her.

He had picked up her slipper and declared he would marry the first woman whose foot could fit into it. That, she thought, was rather strange. Surely there would be any number of women in the kingdom with feet the size of hers. He couldn't really mean to marry just any one of them. And what a ridiculous criterion to begin with. What was it he wanted exactly: her soul, or her sole? She wasn't sure she liked that kind of fetish. But she supposed he did need something to go on, and she really hadn't given him much else.

She wasn't worried, though. That would come later. For now, she felt strangely confident, locked up in her tower, in a way she never had before. Her prince would find her, the shoe would fit her foot – hers alone, for some mysterious reason – and everything would be just the way it was supposed to be; which, she realised, made absolutely no sense whatsoever. But so what if it didn't? It didn't need to make sense. It just needed to work.

Months passed, and people were beginning to lose interest in the prince and his endless quest. Most of them had daughters who had failed the prince's test, or sisters, or they had had the exquisite pleasure of failing it themselves. Even if they hadn't fallen victim to the young man's folly and their own reverie, they could no longer take their future ruler seriously, saying he had gone mad, lost his mind over a woman he would never find.

She, for her part, was growing quite impatient. She didn't know where he was looking, but what was becoming painfully obvious was that he wasn't looking in the right place.

And then, one day, he did.

His carriage pulled up in front of the mansion. It wasn't a particularly sunny day and the birds weren't singing. In fact, it was a rather dark day, mainly owing to the fact that it was a night. It was shortly before pumpkin. Now was the hour of wonders.

She heard her stepmother greet the prince and her throat dried up. She heard him being led into the hall and her heart tried to break out of her chest. She heard her stepsisters' cries of anguish and pain as their mother cut away at their toes in a desperate attempt to make their feet fit the shoe, and her stomach churned and she nearly fainted. Then she heard the prince bidding the household farewell and it occurred to her that she ought to make her presence known.

She yelled. She shouted. She wailed. All to no avail. She kicked. She raged. She … stopped for a moment and thought. She still had the other slipper.

When the prince walked back out into the night, the last thing he expected was to be hit over the head by a falling shoe. The second-to-last thing he expected was for the shoe to be the twin of the one currently hidden away in his chambers in the palace. He looked up. He saw the tower. He smiled. Then he said *ouch* and rubbed his head.

Now was the time of wonders. She didn't utter a word. She knew the prince knew her, but she was determined to go through with the ceremony. She was going to do this right. She would take every step with perfect countenance, smiling inwardly as her stepmother looked on in helpless fury. He presented the shoe for her to step into and, precisely at the hour of the pumpkin …

"That's not my shoe!" she cried out, a cold sensation creeping up from her sole where it touched the glass of the slipper before seizing hold of her entire body and soul.

"Obviously not," he replied, impassive.

"But you don't get it. This is not my shoe. It's not the shoe I was wearing. For crying out loud, this thing is made of glass. How do you suppose I could have been dancing with you wearing glass shoes? It makes absolutely no sense. I'm not the wrong woman; this is the wrong shoe. How stupid are you to think I might have been wearing glass shoes? There's some mistake. THIS IS NOT MY SHOE!"

"There's no mistake."

It was all going awfully wrong. Something had happened. Somehow her stepmother had stolen her pumpkin. She was struggling for air. Then she saw that her prince was laughing.

"Well, you didn't really think you had the smallest feet in all the realm, did you?" He looked awfully pleased with himself. "I'm not a paedophile, you know ... It's a trick. A clever illusion. No one can fit into that shoe. I just needed an excuse for travelling around to look for you ... By the way, did you just call me stupid?"

She told him that, if he didn't want to get slapped, he had better shut up and kiss her. He did. She slapped him anyway. And they lived happily ever after. Well ... until they died.

THE PRINCESS AND THE F***

Am I crazy?

I don't think I am. Would I know if I was?

My name … is a matter of public record. So I don't see why I should write it down. You can look it up, if you want. Sorry. Old habits. I'm sure you know it already. Haven't quite gotten used to that yet.

It's funny, I never quite felt like it belonged to me. It was just what people called me. I'm not complaining. It's not a bad name. No worse than any other. Better than some. Though maybe not any longer.

It was an every-day, every-man, any-man name. Colourless. Meaningless. Flavourless. A respectable name. I'm afraid I haven't done right by it.

Point is, we were never more than roommates, my name and I. Coexisting peacefully, for the most part. And now that it has taken on a life of its own, blitzing from paper to magazine, from radio to television, I barely even recognise it anymore.

So you may refer to me however you like, but don't presume that just because my name is familiar to you, you actually know me. You don't. I'm only slightly acquainted with me myself.

*

The reason I became a cook is because I love to see people happy. Even as a child, I always felt the need to crack a joke or cut a grimace whenever there was tension between my parents or my siblings. Not that it worked. If it had, I might have become a clown. Instead, I started realising that my family was always at its happiest and most relaxed right after a meal.

The castle used to be a merry place following the return of its prince, our beloved King, and his bride-to-be; our late, regretted Queen. When I first started working here, there wasn't one person in the castle's service that would have traded their place for any other. And the cheerfulness only increased with the birth of their first child, our lovely Princess.

Even then, she was a wilful child. Not that it mattered. You expect a child to be difficult. You expect it to want everything and to want it now, right now, no-I-don't-care-if-it's-the-middle-of-the-night-and-everyone-is-sleeping, I want to be fed.

We were more than happy to oblige. I must admit I was no exception. Even in later years, when the wails of the infant turned into the caprices of the girl and the fantasies of the young woman, she could always count on me to enable her every whim. I would cook feasts for her, invent new delicacies, do and redo dishes she had found some fault with, put splendour and sumptuosity ahead of good taste and common sense. And I was never as happy as when she rewarded me with one of her rare smiles.

The King and Queen had always led a simple life and, at first, they made many attempts to dissuade their daughter from some of her more extravagant follies. But they always ended up relenting to their treasure's will … and so it went on.

The country was prosperous, having been governed with wisdom for many years, and the kingdom could afford the excesses of its future ruler. Still, as the royal reserves dwindled and the only heir to the throne showed no signs of settling down, frowns and furrows started to mark the King and Queen's faces, and life in the castle was no longer what it had been.

The day that changed everything was a day like any other. The sun was not shining, but it wasn't raining either. It was a normal day, a greyish sort of day. Only some strange reflection of the sun's distant light lent colour to the sky, soaking the clouds in a kind of orange haze.

The Queen had come down with a sudden fever some days earlier. The King was never the same again. After the state funeral, a grand and solemn affair that seemed to envelop the entire country in its grief, he started withdrawing from the everyday cares of his function. It seemed to make little difference at first but, when it became increasingly apparent that he would no longer perform even the most essential duties of the monarchy, the ministers slowly started to turn towards the Princess for guidance and instructions.

Over the following months, I watched the Princess grow more commanding in her demands, more confident in her eccentricities. Castle life grew ever glummer – its inhabitants perpetually fearful of provoking one of Her Royal Highness' fits, and I feel certain the country suffered as well.

That's when I started to wonder where the King's patience and wisdom had come from, and why it hadn't passed on to his daughter. There had to be some element that would explain the discrepancy in their respective characters.

And then it dawned on me.

The next day, I went to see the fairy godmother. I made my representations to her, and she agreed to help.

*

The changes were subtle at first: a slight sheen of moisture on her hands and forehead, a hoarse quality in her voice, a light hunch in her posture and a discreet wobble in her movements. She was more easily tired now and less quick to flare up in anger. The castle returned to a relative quiet, even if it was still far from the content atmosphere of yonder.

I do not think she minded her transformation much. I do not even think she realised. Her skin took on a greenish hue, her belly grew into a pouch, her entire body started to sag towards the ground and she was forever walking with an awkward slouching, hopping gait – but, in her eyes, she was still the most beautiful maiden in all the land. Then came the warts. When those started appearing, that's when she realised something was seriously wrong.

It didn't take them long to trace the origin of her changes to her favourite soup, and the soup to me. I was the head chef, after all, and the soup had been my last birthday present to her.

I had created it specifically for her benefit and, as an integral part of the present, I hadn't allowed anyone else to taste it. Not just because I didn't want anyone else to suffer the effects, which was true, but because I had known that this very fact would appeal to her, and this, more than the soup's taste – it was rather bland, to be honest – was the reason why she was soon calling for her special soup every day.

They were rather shocked to discover what some of the soup's ingredients were. The hunting and consuming of frogs was forbidden, after all, and had been ever since the Queen's kiss had brought the King back from his existence amongst them. Strangely, the fact that I had drawn inspiration from His Majesty's own education, and had tried to afford his daughter the same curriculum, didn't seem to weigh in my favour in the proceedings that followed.

*

There are footsteps in the corridor leading up to my cell. Small and Heavy. I'm sure they have names as well, but that's how I refer to them. Small is explaining how "Mrs Robinson" was written for that Dustin Hoffmann movie by *The Lemonheads*. Heavy reacts with unfeigned awe. Morons.

"Wakey, wakey!" trumpets Small – he always does that; no use trying to explain we're in the middle of the afternoon and I wasn't sleeping. "Time for your medical!"

Right. Because, before they can kill me, they have to make sure I'm in perfect health. The King vetoed a law on euthanasia a few years back. If you want help dying, you have to commit a heinous crime and be at the peak of your capabilities … physical capabilities, that is. No one cares if you're clinically insane; which, again, I do not believe I am.

I wait for the perfect moment, when they're no longer paying any attention to me – which doesn't really take very long, truth be told – and then ram my heel against Small's shin. He swears. I grin. Heavy whacks me over the head.

"That was for Paul Simon," I tell him.

"Nutjob," he tells me.

I've spent my life trying to make people happy. I feel a surge of smug satisfaction at my new-found pettiness.

*

I am due to be executed in the morning. The King is a good chap, as I said, but apparently the transformation of his only daughter into an amphibian was not something he could overlook.

So this is it. My road ends here.

But, in the meantime, the Princess' transformation is complete, and I feel strangely happy about it all.

POSTCONTEMPORARY BEAUTY

In spite of the new systemic regulator, Miss Evelyn-Rachel Theodora Fairmother-Stepbottom had turned in a rather fitful resting performance and, when she switched into interactive mode that month (two days late, as it were), she felt positively and determinedly indignant. Positively and determinedly indignant at whom or what she couldn't have told you, but positively and determinedly indignant it was.

"Up," she mouthed, and her cocoon unfolded and sank into the bowels of the mansion, while she was risen from the waters in slowly rotating majesty, until she reached her usual position at an angle of 54.9 degrees. She sneezed. The room temperature should have been an exact 27.8 degrees, but she was feeling a slight chill, and immediately had it augmented with an impatient flicker of her eyelid. Her skin was sucked clear of chemical dredges, then embalmed and dried by electromagnetic radiation. She had a syringe for sustainment (guaranteed free of long-term nutrition), swallowed a few drops of hydrating fluid (one of the pink ones; she only ever had the pink ones) and had her mouth disinfected before calling for her dressmaker.

The man's head materialised in mid-air, but it appeared she had caught him at an inopportune time, and it took several coughs before he finally took notice of his audience. Slightly annoyed, the face stopped gasping and gave a grunt in her general direction.

"Driss," she hissed at him, and the slight annoyance gave way to proper dismay.

"Oh, honey," he sighed, "they didn't inform you."

Miss Evelyn-Rachel Theodora Fairmother-Stepbottom croaked something back at him.

"I didn't get that," said the head, "and, frankly, I no longer care. You no longer work for us; ergo, I no longer work for you. You can find your own dress."

Miss Evelyn-Rachel Theodora Fairmother-Stepbottom coughed in protest.

"Sorry darling, but that's just the way it is. And, quite frankly, you should have seen it coming. I mean, for beauty's sake, woman, have some decency. You're nineteen years old! You have been the face of our company for almost seven years. You've had a terrific run, but it's time to move on. You're getting old, sweetie. Nobody wants to see your tired body anymore. Female beauty was never meant to last that long." And, just when Miss Evelyn-Rachel Theodora Fairmother-Stepbottom thought things couldn't possibly get any worse, he added, "I mean, just look at yourself, woman. Look at your scalp: you're growing hair!"

Miss Evelyn-Rachel Theodora Fairmother-Stepbottom's replacement turned out to be rather old herself, which only served to increase the disavowed beauty queen's fury. Still, at a respectable fifteen years of age, Miss Bianca Hallelujah Blackflake-Snowmane the Younger was undoubtedly still a beauty. Her latest operation had only served to increase her already impressive ethereality. And, as Miss Evelyn-Rachel Theodora Fairmother-Stepbottom's Mirroar™ had put it, "Not even Michael Jackson was ever that white." That was when she had decided that the harlot that had taken her place had to be stopped.

"Appls," she spat at the Mirroar™, and the Mirroar™, personified, as per Miss Evelyn-Rachel Theodora Fairmother-Stepbottom's instructions, as her own perfect face, replied – in someone else's perfect diction – "Apples? Certainly, my lady. Any preference?"

To which she in turn replied, "Fckshim."

Thus it was that, when Miss Bianca Hallelujah Blackflake-Snowmane the Younger finally awoke from her slumber some days later (for thus is the privilege of beauty), she found her hydrating fluid – made, like those of everyone-who-mattered, by Deerhunter Corporations – to have a peculiar, though not at all unpleasant aftertaste. It might be of some noteworthiness at this point that the Right Honourable Mister Deerhunter had previously been sued over some unfortunate incidents of poisoning, and had been in a very uncomfortable position indeed before being resurrected by the sudden interest of Miss Evelyn-Rachel Theodora Fairmother-Stepbottom, who had found him to produce the loveliest shades of pink. Miss Bianca Hallelujah Blackflake-Snowmane the Younger, however, preferred her hydrating fluids to be green, and was absolutely delighted by the new fluorescent prototype Deerhunter had developed for her; absolutely delighted, that is, until the Fukushima apples took effect. And that, ladies and gentlemen, was that.

*

Or it would have been, were it not for Miss Bianca Hallelujah Blackflake-Snowmane the Younger's younger sister, the redoubtable Miss Bianca Hallelujah Blackflake-Snowmane the Youngest, who insisted that her sibling and role-model's unmatched ethereality was a work of art and artful artifice (she was rather plump herself, weighing all of thirty-seven kilograms, and had always insisted that it-was-a-virtue-not-a-failing-and-that-too-much-was-too-much-thank-you-very-much!) and that, as such, it belonged on public display and would certainly attract a procession of pious admirers.

Thus it was that, despite the vehement protestations of some ancient beauty queen — a woman by the name of *Stepmother-Fairbottom*, or something – Miss Bianca Hallelujah Blackflake-Snowmane the Younger was auctioned off to the Museum of Postcontemporary Art, a winner over the Right Honourable Society for the Consumption of Incarnate Beauty stewed in Mint Sauce (RHSfCIBsMS), for the modest sum of a-shitload-of-money – a deal that had entailed Miss Bianca Hallelujah Blackflake-Snowmane the Youngest's willingness to allow the director of the institute, a rather diminutive man with a peculiar interest in famous people's relatives, and his six equally diminutive co-workers, to stroke her naked bottom and spank her once-each-but-not-too-hard. The director insisted on recording the whole process on his phone, citing academic reasons, which hadn't originally been agreed upon, but she wasn't going to risk the deal by protesting this close to her a-shitload-of-money (though why the seven of them would want to perform any of the aforementioned actions, she couldn't possibly conceive). She was however dismayed to find that her underpants were no longer to be found once the transaction had been completed in good and proper form.

The director gave his new acquisition a central spot at the beating heart – or so he persisted in saying – of his exhibition, deciding to display it in all its naked splendour – for a more genuine experience, he insisted, and an experience it was – enclosed behind a wall of glass, preserved from decay and the general passage of time for all eternity – and wasn't that just the dream, he kept asking his visitors by way of several gigantic holograms; wasn't that just the dream?

Miss Bianca Hallelujah Blackflake-Snowmane the Younger might have agreed – she was, after all, fast becoming the epitome of ethereal beauty – but, whether or not she shared her new owner's vision of what her dream world might look like, the man himself was certainly enjoying a dream of his own. Never before had one of his exhibits drawn so many viewers. He was now giving interviews on a regular basis, winning prizes for his role in Furthering the Advancement of the Arts and Western Lifestyle. One reporter had even called him the first Postcontemporary Feminist – something that had made him chuckle at first, but which he had lately started to believe in himself. It beat being called a pedantic dwarf, and the sales of Bianca Hallelujah Blackflake-Snowmane-the-Younger-related materials were *insane*.

Which is why when, after being alerted by an outraged and rightfully disgusted viewer, he found himself unable to further ignore the dreadful reality; namely, that his chef-d'œuvre had begun to develop some strange protrusions on her previously immaculate chest, the manner in which he failed to ignore it was pervaded by a not inconsequential measure of despondency. At first, he tried to hide these new developments, shaving the hair his masterpiece was starting to grow in strange places – above the eyes, for example, or between her legs – and changing the light to hide her gaining of weight. But the protrusions were simply too much to bear. The director made a last-ditch attempt to sell his acquisition on to the Right Honourable Society for the Consumption of Incarnate Beauty stewed in Mint Sauce (RHSfCIBsMS), but found that they would no longer take her in her current form. Under the gaze of her not-so-secretly elated younger sister, Miss Bianca Hallelujah Blackflake-Snowmane the Younger was finally moved to the Cabinet of Horrors, Oddities and Aberrations, there to be forgotten by all who could– the director himself still having the occasional nightmare about her.

It was a long time before the once so admired beauty queen sparked any kind of public interest again, though she did establish a cult following amongst lovers of the macabre and the perverse. One day, however, as fate would have it, the local university was visited by the great academic Professor Prince who, out of boredom perhaps, also took a quick tour of the museum. While he was less than impressed with the permanent collection, and even less impressed by the current special exhibit (dedicated to the Extraordinary Beauty of All Things Small), he was quite taken aback when he finally stumbled upon the dusty glass that still encapsulated Miss Bianca Hallelujah Blackflake-Snowmane the Younger's increasingly exuberant flesh.

No other man in the country could have understood what he felt then. Could it possibly be …? No, surely not. And yet … where another man could only have seen malformation, Professor Prince – being a student of Pre-Postcontemporary Art – had to conclude … unmistakably … that he was in the presence of three perfectly formed female breasts.

It was while she was being moved from the museum to Professor Prince's residence that Miss Bianca Hallelujah Blackflake-Snowmane the Younger finally regained consciousness. Later, no one in the medical community would be able to comprehend how she could have been pronounced dead by poisoning in the first place, as there hadn't been much of her left to poison to begin with (though there was somewhat more of her now). Nor had there been any reason to believe her dead since, as for a beauty queen of her ethereality, six months of coma weren't really that much, all things considered, and neither were six months of food deprivation, and she had been sipping a rather powerful hydrating fluid right before her nap.

Professor Prince was at first dumbfounded by this new development, but he soon decided to make her a proposition she couldn't refuse (she was, after all, his property, having legally been sold by her sister to the Museum of Postcontemporary Art and by said museum to Professor Prince). They had the most splendid wedding ceremony, though her sister made a point of outmatching her in every way six months later, when she married the director and all of his assistants. They had been fired from the museum for their exhibition on the

Extraordinary Beauty of All Things Small, but landed on their feet, dedicating themselves to conducting innovative bio-physical experiments on the female body, using their new bride as their main (and only) test subject. As for Miss Evelyn-Rachel Theodora Fairmother-Stepbottom, Mistress Bianca Hallelujah Blackflake-Snowmane-Prince exercised some small measure of revenge against her by sending her a pair of shoes so small, not even she could fit into them.

BLUEBEARD

My beard is blue,
My lips are red,
My coat is fine and trendy.

My heart is gold,
My conscience white,
My only vice is brandy.

While say they may —
What may one say? —
Words vile and false and spiteful …

What deeds are mine,
Well, dare I say,
Were all well-meant and rightful.

A wife I had,
A precious thing,
But fragile as a flower –

A fever came,
She lay in pain,
I shortened her last hour.

She may have died,
By mine own hand,
But god knows it was mercy.

Though all they see
Is – that makes three!
They still remember Lucy.

Now Lucy was
A girl well liked,
The prettiest on the border.

She could have lived,
I chose the child,
And lost both child and mother.

It's funny though,
They do say three,
They suddenly remember.

When Lily died,
My one true love,
Not one did seek her killer.

My last wife's death
Left me bereft,
And also in some bother;

No woman left
Would take her place,
Not one but her dear sister.

She came one day
And simply said,
We still need your allegiance –

I didn't know,
But really though,
What she came for was vengeance.

I married her.
I made her mine.
My own grave I was digging.

I gave her keys,
She gave me lies,
And kept one room for knitting.

She spent her days,
Some nights as well,
Locked up in total darkness —

I never asked
On what she worked;
She said it'd leave me breathless.

We never spoke,
Met but in bed,
But there, my god, were restless:

She made me beat
And whip her hard.
I thought it all quite harmless.

I must admit
I didn't mind;
At long last I was merry.

It wasn't quite
Like Lily's days,
But still those days were happy.

Then came the morn,
She looked forlorn –
I was by now besotten.

She looked at me …
It's been a year …
It had – I had forgotten.

It'd been a year
Since Annie's death,
And we had to remember.

We threw a feast,
I drank a lot;
I must have – can't remember.

I soon woke up
To shouts and cries;
At me they were all looking.

I looked around,
And what I saw,
My last breath shall be haunting.

The skeletons
Of all my wives
In wide array were sitting.

I even saw
My baby child;
With blood my beard was glistening.

She spoke up then,
With tranquil voice,
And yet I felt compassion.

I feared her then
And yet enjoyed
Her graceful composition.

He killed them all,
My sister Anne
And Lucy and the baby.

And quite a few
We never knew,
That monster knows no pity.

I'm telling you,
He is a beast,
A killer and a rapist.

On that last note,
She dropped her coat;
She had the scars to prove it.

They took me then,
They dragged me out,
Away from my wife's knitting.

And while they pulled
I caught a glance,
At last my wife was smiling.

My end is nigh,
The branch is high,
And none of them are listening.

They're beating me,
And kicking me,
And some of them are whistling.

They're jolly now,
They're dancing now,
And most of them are singing …

They're giggling now,
And pointing now,
And all of them are grinning.

And still I kick,
And still I cry,
I never saw it coming.

Despite the spurn,
Despite the spite,
I never saw it coming.

I swear to them
It was not so,
As god shall be my witness.

I swear and swear
It is not so,
And all of you are god—

THE BEAUTY OF THE BEAST

I am a man, and a man takes what he wants.

I am a prince, and a prince does not speak; he acts.

I am a hunter, and I always get what I want.

The pedlar was old and tired, cold and frightened. He did not make for good game. In truth he was not worthy of my time, but I was bored and I had little else to do. I am not a cruel man, and I do not kill my prey, except for food, or sport. So I chased him not to catch him – which I could have done in an instant – but to see him run, and I chased him towards my castle, not towards the ravine, or deeper into the woods where he would get lost and freeze to death during the night. I was going to make him run, be my distraction for the night, but there would be a meal waiting for him, and a bed, in recompense. He was getting more than his due, truth be told. I was feeling rather generous under the moonlight.

The rose was one of a kind. It was the most exquisite I had ever grown. It was beauty. It was art. It was blood-made-petal, tooth-made-thorn. So when the old man broke its perfect neck and it sank its tooth into his thumb – one last desperate act of revenge – when the fragrance of the old man's blood filled my nostrils and woke me from my peaceful slumber, and I understood what he had done, it only took an instant for my teeth to kiss his throat, the sharp points drawing his blood one last time as my powerful jaws crushed his bones, snapped his spine and twisted his face around in one smooth motion. I left the head where it fell, but dragged the body away and had my fill of it.

I never gave the incident another thought.

A more sentimental man, to be sure, might have felt regret for the loss of his garden's most precious ornament, but I am not one to dwell on the past. Regret will not bring back the moonshine of yesternight. I had suffered a loss; had, in fact, been robbed. But the thief had been punished; justice had been done. It would have been most unbecoming to waste another moment on a situation that had, for all intents and purposes, already found its proper resolution.

So when *she* came asking for her father, I did not at first perceive the correlation. I listened to her politely, half bored and half aroused. She made quite the striking apparition, despite her calloused hands and sunburnt skin. The peasant in her was quite apparent to my eyes, one need not say, but there was also something else in her. Beneath her scruffy exterior, some innate quality seemed to be shining through. In the shape of her neck, the curve of her hips, there was ... something. Now if I could just get her out of that dreadful garb, rectify some of the damage of her wretched lifestyle, she might make for an acceptable distraction. I agreed to help her in her quest.

It was not love at first sight.

I did not know what I was getting myself into – not yet – but it certainly did not start out as a romance. I had killed the dogs long ago, so there was no other way to look for the old man than to comb the woods on foot. I did not mind: I liked watching her walk, her hips swaying ever so gently from side to side. There was no exaggeration, no eccentricity in her movements. I became quite entranced by the slight rise and rapid fall of her skirt with every step she took. I was surprised by the amount of details I took in from her demeanour, but she was quite unlike any girl I had met so far, and I had been quite bored the past few days.

We spent the rest of that day battling through the undergrowth, searching under every bush, shouting for her father to make his position known. I was sceptical, but she would not allow herself to abandon hope. So I applied myself to the task at hand with renewed ardour, making sure she marked the extent of my efforts. I climbed trees, I moved rocks, I crawled through caves, I let my voice ring throughout the woods, making a show of my strength and dexterity, as well as my good will and noble spirit. It did not go unnoticed. At last, with the light failing, I convinced her to come back to the castle, arguing that we would have better luck in the morn, when I could go and get help from the village.

It was all going according to plan.

On the way back, I applied myself to cheering her up. I jested and I wheedled and I cajoled. I applied all my wit and all my charm and, at last, I had coaxed a smile from her – when her glance fell upon a familiar object beneath the roses.

The old man was still recognisable, despite the onset of decay. I saw the smile freeze on her lips, and I understood. She looked at me as if she was seeing me for the first time. The horror in her eyes, the frailty of her frame, seemed to indicate she would break down at the slightest urge, yet there was so much defiance in her stance it took my breath away, and I hardly dared to move myself. She might break, but she would not bow. That was when I made up my mind that I had to have her.

It would have been easy to take her there and then, but already I wanted more; wanted her to want me; wanted her to be mine, body and soul. So I locked her in the castle's very best apartments, excepting mine. I started an elaborate courtship, the likes of which a simple girl like her could never have dreamed of. I fed her delicacies the existence of which she could never have imagined. I showed her wonders she could never have conceived of. I plied and showered her with the most eccentric gifts.

She never said a word to me.

I was, I will concede, somewhat taken aback by her obstinacy. But this only served to excite me even more. I truly had never met a girl like her before. No woman has ever resisted me so. Sure, I had not been very social since … the incident, but I prided myself on having had quite the hand with girls before. Few could withstand my charms, fewer my riches, and none, of course, my sheer physical power. But I was not going to resort to that with her. Nor had it been my favourite manner of proceeding in days of old, not as long as there was another way of obtaining satisfaction … though I will admit to a certain lack of patience having manifested itself in my dealings with the fairer sex ever since the change first came upon me.

It began to dawn on me that I would never win her affections with any treasure mined or forged from here to the Blue Mountains. I had to think of a better way. It might have taken me a while to find the right approach, but I do declare I am rather proud of what I came up with in the end. In later years I have come to think of it as the best battle plan I ever laid down. And, dear me, did it ever end in triumph …

I started revealing a more fragile side of the beast to her. The fact that I was making it up as I went along was in no way detrimental to the effect it produced on my target. On the contrary, it allowed me to tailor my new identity to the form of her very soul. I am a fine observer, you must know. True power uses every means at its disposal, it does not limit itself to brute force. I do not believe in the sanctity of the human being – man is just another animal – but if there was something separating us from the lion ¡or the wolf, it would be this: the art of warfare begins with the subjugation of physical violence to the power of the intellect.

Hence it is for a girl I rediscovered the art of poem and song. It is for her I discovered the pleasure of tears shed. It is her who showed me the immense power of frailty. But this was not just a study – and gradual transformation – of my own self. I learned everything there was to know about her. Things she herself did not even suspect. I learned what made her heart beat faster; I learned what made her eyes mist over; I learned what made her shrink and what made her quiver. It is incredible what power you can acquire over an individual by learning their deepest fears and their most profound desires.

I bade my time.

I spent months preparing her. She never knew a thing, obviously. She just seemed glad of the ceasefire I had gradually brought her to accept. Not that she had forgiven anything – never that – nor had she forgotten. Neither the fate of her father nor her own situation were ever far from her mind, and she still flinched whenever I entered a room she had thought herself to be alone in. But she had seen what she perceived to be my weaknesses, and she no longer thought me a monster. She had not tried to escape for several weeks, growing accustomed to the comfort of her captivity.

It helped that she had nowhere to return to.

I made sure she started to think of the castle as home, going as far as tracking down her old house – if such a poor and unadorned hovel can be called a house – and adding discreet touches of it to her apartments and the common areas. I even added some paternal overtones to the design of my own personality. I also made sure to move as many carriable valuables as I could to the main entrance hall, in anticipation of later developments, though I will admit the exact form of these were still somewhat vague to me at that point. I took her for walks throughout my lands, regaling her with the spectacular panoramas and the hidden gems, making her fall for my country, if not for my own person. I had the pack attack us during one of these promenades, just so she could see me defend her against ravenous wolves at what must have seemed like great peril to myself.

What I had not expected was for her to cry out not in fear for her life, but when an overeager stripling actually drew some blood from my own veins, forcing me to snap its neck in retaliation. The wound was shallow and of no real import, but she insisted on washing and binding it. For a moment, I stopped being the enemy, instead appearing as a fellow human being in need of her help. I did not disabuse her of the notion. I let her care for me, seeing the way forward more clearly than I ever had before.

You would be surprised how easily I can plant an idea in someone's head. Man is a suggestible animal, and I have always excelled at getting people to do my bidding. The eagerness of humans to submit to a superior power – be it through conscious action or in more subtle ways – is truly astonishing. Sometimes it scares even me.

The village hero was not a particularly bright individual. He had a square jaw, fair hair, chiselled arms and all the other typical attributes you expect in your average human hero. His smile was larger than his head. I had often observed him venturing into my woods, going farther than any of his comrades ever would, always on the lookout for a prize worthy of his claim. I found him most amusing. Once, I had chanced upon him as he followed a stag too deeply into the greens, getting cornered between the pack and the ravine. He would have perished then, were it not for me. So, even though he did not know it, his life was already mine by rights.

I decided it was time he paid his debt.

I took malicious pleasure in haunting the village over the following weeks, killing sheep, dogs and the occasional cow or horse, breaking fences and chariots … I even went so far as to attack the church one night, leaving the local priest in a helpless bundle, scared half to death, having wetted his robe, convinced he had been besieged by all the demons of hell.

The hero tracked me easily enough. I had made sure I left marks aplenty, and all he had to do was follow them. He did so with meticulous care, certain that my path would eventually lead him to my cave, my grove, some great beast's lair ... He did not expect a castle. Nevertheless, when he had made certain the tracks did not lead anywhere but to the front porch, he started looking for a way in, working quickly and in total silence, never suspecting his quarry was quietly observing him from the border of the wood he had just left behind.

I saw them meet, heard them talk, every word of it distinct to me over the meadow. It appeared like a perfectly rehearsed play to me, fitting my purpose as seamlessly as if I had scripted it myself. She called out to him from her window, too narrow and too high to escape through. He vowed to save her and queried after the hound or wolf or trained bear that was being kept here. She assured him there was no beast in the castle, save for its master. I could smell her blush as she said this, and she looked away from her would-be-rescuer with a guilty expression, and I knew I was on the right track.

He applied himself to his task with renewed ardour, making sure she marked the extent of his efforts. He tried climbing the wall, knocking on rocks, crawling through the overgrown bushes that bordered the castle walls, making a show of his strength and flexibility, as well as his good will and determination. At last, with the light failing, he convinced her to let him leave for the night, arguing that he would have better luck in the morn, when he could return with help from the village ...

They posted guards.

They rebuilt the fences, fortified them to the best of their abilities.

They built up fires against the night.

I do not make mistakes very often, but the very perfection of my own abilities had made me overestimate the extent of his. I had misjudged his hold over the villagers, and so had he. After all, a hero's smile is so much more winning when he does not require you to follow him into danger … They had no intention of following me into my forest. But there was no keeping me out, and there was no keeping me in. Sooner or later, they would have to take the bait.

It was the child that settled it, the hero's daughter. I had had no plan of harming her. I was out on my usual rampage, creating as much chaos as I could, laughing at the villagers running around in circles behind me, when she suddenly jumped out into the street. I froze. She froze. She looked at me with big round eyes, undecided between panic and delight. She was a beautiful child, with her big round face and her small pointy nose. She extended her hand towards my head. I reacted almost by instinct.

I left her hand clearly visible on the road, her finger pointing the way towards my castle.

They came with shovels and pitchforks, with crossbows and torches. They came with their pain and their anger, and the desire to kill. There were about two-score of them. The show was finally about to begin.

She, of course, thought it was all her own doing, and she was afraid they would do me harm. I enquired whether that would pain her. She blushed and replied she abhorred violence against any living being. She would not meet my eyes as she said this. Even as she spoke the truth, she made for a pitiful liar.

That is the moment I chose to break down in tears.

I told her I could lie to her no more. I told her I was cursed with a terrible affliction, one passed down to me through generations, and that there lived a beast inside of me I could not at all times control. I told her my father had been a hard and cruel man, and that it was his blood inside of me turned me into a beast.

It was not all lies. My procreator really had been a hard and cruel man, and the beast really did come to me from his blood, and the blood of his father, and his father's father, through generations unknown. But if there was one thing I did not resent him for, it was precisely the gift of strength he had bestowed upon me. But I did not tell her that. I also did not tell her how the man had died.

For a moment she said nothing, and I feared I had miscalculated. Then they started hammering on the doors, and she gave a shriek. She implored me to run, to not let them find me here, to not give them a chance to hurt me.

That made me laugh. Did she really think any of them could lay a finger on me if I did not want them to? I am a killer, trained for war. Even without my gift, without the use of any weapon other than my perfect physical mould, without resorting to the assistance of the pack, or to the many defences, natural or otherwise, of the castle itself, how long did she think it would take me to dispatch that ridiculous hero of hers? And how long did she imagine the rabble would stand firm after I had disembowelled their leader?

I was about to signify as much, but I caught myself just in time, and I managed to turn my triumphant howl into a bitter growl. I told her I had to face my destiny, that no one can escape judgement forever, and that I would not shrink back from my accusers. She told me they would kill me. I told her that perhaps it was exactly what I deserved, that perhaps it would be for the best. I assured her I would not fight back, would not harm any of the villagers in my own defence.

She looked more disconsolate than ever.

I did not give her time to come up with a reply and mar my perfect moment of self-sacrifice, but released the charm protecting the doors, allowing the peasants to come crashing into my reception hall. For a moment, there was stunned silence. Then the hero's voice rang through the castle, challenging me to show myself. I started walking towards his voice, moving with all the gravitas befitting the apparent earnestness of the occasion, as well as my own lofty station, hiding away my excitement at what was to come, treating the pleas of my desolate audience with all the disdain and arrogant countenance of a Roman hero.

When we arrived down the hall, the pillage had already begun. Here again my calculations had proven correct: my simple enticement had overwhelmed the peasants' puny minds. Only the hero had remained attentive, clad in his pain and fury. To my astonishment, he had managed to procure an actual sword from somewhere, which he now raised against me. I applauded inwardly. The theatrics were perfect.

I landed one punch, just the one, to shatter his jaw and prevent him from whining about his daughter. Then, as if suddenly remembering my promise, I joined my hands behind my back and kept them there, visibly fighting not to retaliate, while I let him drive me back with savage strokes of his rustic blade, his furious desperation nothing more than blind hatred in her eyes. Around us, the pillage was turning into wanton destruction, and I knew it was only a matter of time before one of the peasants turned his attentions towards the real prize … It is always thus with unbloodied soldiers.

There were three of them, in the end, cornering her between the gilded handrail of the main stairway and a heavy ebony cabinet. It was the chance I had been waiting for. I howled, and while I howled, I turned and changed, and already I had thrown the hero aside with the back of my left paw. One jump was all it took to bring me amongst her assailants.

I bore down on them like the Vengeance of God.

I made such short work of them that, by the time

I caught the terror in her eyes, and remembered I was supposed to get wounded in my gallant effort to rescue her, there was already no one left to oblige. I paused. I made an attempt at an apologetic smile – not a simple feat in my current manifestation – but she was looking beyond me.

I felt the blade enter my back like a shard of ice.

The hero.

Sh–

I fell at her feet. Out of the corner of my eye, I saw his face light up in heinous triumph, its expression a mockery of joy with the dislocated jaw and the broken teeth. It seemed he had been waiting for his opportunity as well. It seemed he had known I was but toying with him. It seemed I had underestimated him, letting myself be distracted. Do not take your eyes off your prey ... but she had been my prey, not him. I was at his mercy then. He raised his sword over his head.

She threw herself between us.

I could hear them struggle as I crawled away, the noises of the scuffle intermingling with her woeful cries and his ireful groans. I got back up when I reached the doors, forcing myself forward on trembling legs. I no longer knew where I was going, but the scent of the roses caught my nose, and I found myself following it through the gardens.

I went down between the simple grave that had received the bones of *her* father and the mausoleum that would never see the bones of *mine*.

It was her touch that woke me, her face that greeted my opening eyes. She was covered in blood, but she seemed unharmed. I had never seen a more delicious sight. She looked concerned. I wanted to laugh. Instead, for the first time in … for the first time … I cried. I do not know how long we stayed thus, her frail arms holding my massive frame. I kept trying to apologise, though for what I did not know.

She kissed me.

I had a moment of insanity. For a moment, the world made sense. For a moment, I knew the meaning of life, and all was as it should be. I came to my senses just in time, realising the importance of the opportunity. I returned her embrace, threw myself into her kiss and, at its paroxysm, I let the wolf slip away.

It was a full moon. I had chosen my perfect moment perfectly.

The rest was easy. I had been liberated from my curse, I told her. The village hero had slain the beast, but she had brought the man back to life. We were wed soon after, and we have been living happily ever since. We even have a baby daughter. She is a beautiful child, with her big round face and her small pointy nose …

I do not worry about her discovering the truth. I am fairly certain she already knows, though I do not believe she would ever admit to it. But she always knows when to give me space. So, when the moon calls out to me, or when I feel like stretching my legs, I do not even need to make up an excuse. She just retreats to her chambers, locking the doors behind her. She takes to her chambers a lot these days. She always takes our daughter with her. Foolish girl. As if I would ever hurt the child. After all, I will need someone to carry the bloodline, if the mother fails to give me a son.

It amuses me that I now have a family of my own. Father would be so proud. I never thought I was the marrying type, but it all works out quite well. You just have to find the right balance, and the right partner. Someone who knows when to be there, and when to look away. The secret of a successful marriage lies in respecting your partner's little secrets.

She has her monthly bleedings, and I have mine.

FOREWORD

Let me start by apologising.

Putting an afterword at the front and a foreword at the back of a book is not particularly clever or novel, nor is it entirely respectful. But I wanted to write a foreword, and I wanted you to not feel obligated to read it first. The work should speak for itself. Hence the foreword at the end. Balance then demanded an afterword at the beginning.[1] Which in turn meant I had to move one story in front of it because, again, the work should speak for itself. Does that mean that the foreword and afterword are not really part of the book? Look, if I start explaining myself, we'll never get to the end of it.

The reason I wanted to include a foreword is threefold: I wanted to introduce myself and the place I call home.[2]

---

1. Though, truth be told, while the foreword at the back is a foreword at the back, the afterword at the front is really just another foreword. But that's neither here nor there.
2. It can't be helped. I happen to be a tour guide.

I wanted to pass on some information I wish I had been given when I was starting out,[3] and I wanted to mark the moment of my first standalone publication by just briefly stepping out of my role as the unseen presence behind the text and saying hello.

about me

I'm a strange one, but I shall try and explain nevertheless.

First, the hair:

I'm not a rocker, and I'm not a biker, though I like rock (but not as much as I like jazz), and I like … bicycles. I'm not John Lennon's ghost either. You don't want me to try your ears with my version of Imagine. Trust me. I simply like my hair that way, that's all (except when it's trying to strangle me in my sleep). I'm fifty percent hair and fifty percent hat. Everything else is contingency. Look, I don't ask you to explain your hairdo, do I? In fact, I'll now explicitly ask you not to. There, that should do it.

Second, the name:

My name is Jean.[4] That being said, I'll also present myself as Jang, John, Juan, Giovanni … I am translatable, even as no language can define me on its own.

My surname is of no concern.[5] Suffice it to say that it

____

3. Meaning now. Starting out is exactly what I'm doing here.

4. Et non Jean-Planplan ou Jean-tout-court ou Jean-tout-seul. Jean. Juste Jean. Merde, quoi.

5. That, and Beurlet. The name's **Beurlet. Jean Beurlet.**

starts with the letter B and, although currently of French shape and spelling, is presumed to be derived from the Italian word *burla*. That's according to research by a family cousin and, since I rather like that etymology, I tend to agree.

As it happens, I'm actually not French. Or Italian. I'm something far stranger than that. I'm a Luxembourger. So, seeing as my first name was already French, I obviously needed a Germanic surname to re-establish the balance. That's why Bürlesk has a German spelling. Trust me, it does make sense.

about us

Luxembourg is the world's only remaining grand duchy. It lies between France, Germany and Belgium, and its 2,586km² is home to a population of 614,000. Some of us even have the nationality. In fact, there are slightly more than 320,000 Luxembourgers, the rest of the population being composed of about 95,000 Portuguese, 45,000 French, 22,500 Italians, 20,000 Belgians, 13,000 Germans, and so on and so forth. The British population is decreasing as, for some mysterious reason, many of them are now taking on Luxemburgish nationality.[6] Add to this almost 200,000 people travelling in from France,

---

6. This was actually a major factor in the percentage of Luxembourgers amongst the total population increasing between January 2018 and 2019 for the first time in … forever.

Germany and Belgium to work in Luxembourg every day, and you get a very multicultural and multilingual place.

The national language, the one we Luxembourgers speak amongst ourselves, is Luxembourgish. *Wann ech lo Lëtzebuergesch mat Iech schwätzen, da versti Dir warscheinlech net vill, ausser Dir sidd selwer Lëtzebuerger natierlech, oder Däitsch, dat geet och nach deelweis ...* The point being that you won't get very far with that alone, which is why every Luxembourger speaks at least four languages: Luxembourgish (of course), along with German and French, being the languages of our great neighbours, and English as an international language.[7] There are not nearly enough Luxembourgers learning Portuguese.

Now, when I said I wanted to introduce you to my home, the place I really meant was the city of Luxembourg, more than the country. Not that I don't love the country – I do – I just don't believe in it. Neither should you. Countries are borders. I do believe in the state of Luxembourg – it keeps me from getting strangled by my neighbour – but I do not believe in the nation. That's a religion that has killed far too many people. I shall not tell you about my city here. There are too many things to say and too little space to do it. Instead, I'll tell

---

7. I myself am quite fluent in Spanish as well, am currently playing around with Italian, Portuguese and Russian, hoping to add them to the collection at some point. If only I wasn't so lazy.

the best thing about my country: we're too small and too multicultural to think of ourselves as the one true nation.

about them

I never used to have a favourite writer, or a favourite book (not since the one with the rabbit. I loved the one with the rabbit. No idea what it was about except, conceivably, a rabbit, but I know I used to carry it with me everywhere, before I started walking and talking and all that other nonsense). Until one day I did, and her name was J. K. Rowling. She ruined everything.

If you were to ask me for a book that changed my life, *Harry Potter and the Philosopher's Stone* would probably top the list.[8] It just didn't necessarily change my life for the better. Before Rowling, I read anything and everything. After Rowling, all I wanted to read was fantasy. Not that I'm complaining about fantasy as a genre – some of the books I read during that period I will cherish forever[9] – but I believe that self-imposed restriction is part of what years later led to me reading less and less, until only

---

8. Along with the book about the rabbit, the *Collected Works of William Shakespeare* and something by Neil Gaiman, not quite sure what – *Neverwhere* maybe, or his short story collections.
9. Cornelia Funke (*Drachenreiter*), Tonke Dragt (*De brief voor de koning, Geheimen van het Wilde Woud* – in German, since I don't speak or read Dutch) and Lian Hearn (first in French, and later in English) are particular standouts.

drama kept me in the game.[10] It took *A Song of Ice and Fire* to get me reading fantasy again. And it took Neil Gaiman to get me writing it again.

Neil Gaiman was a revelation. He reminded me I loved fantasy, in particular legends and fairy tales. He reminded me I loved humour, especially dark humour and British humour. He convinced me that I wanted to, and could, write in English, rather than French or German. And he showed what a great medium short stories could be. The result is the book you're currently holding in your hands.

about this

The stories in this collection were conceived and written between 2014 and 2018, when I submitted them to the Servais Foundation. Now if you're not a Luxembourger, you probably won't have heard of the Servais Foundation before, but to Luxembourg's literary landscape, it is of paramount importance. Its most visible manifestation lies in the Servais Prize, Luxembourg's equivalent of the Booker Prize, awarded to the best book of the previous year, ever since I was born.[11] To date, it has been awarded 28 times, rewarding books written by Luxembourgish nationals or residents in Luxembourgish (8), German

---

10. From Molière, Racine and Edmond Rostand, through Shakespeare and Wilde, to Schiller and Kleist as well as Ibsen and every Russian playwright whose name isn't Chekhov.
11. 1992. No causal link as far as I know.

(12),[12] French (7), or all three languages at once (1).

I didn't win that, in case you were wondering. Not yet, anyway. I would have to publish something first. But the Servais Foundation also occasionally awards an Encouragement Prize for the best unpublished first manuscript, and that's where *The Pleasure of Drowning* comes in.[13]

This book was always going to be called *The Pleasure of Drowning*. Before any of the stories it contains were written, the title was already clear in my mind. I like that title. It might be the best thing about the book.[14] I put Mearns' *Antigonish* at the head of the book because I find it both genuinely beguiling and profoundly disturbing. I feel the same about the title. If my stories sometimes strike that same balance, I have achieved what I set out to do.

Hair

This is my calling card. If I have just a few minutes to read something, this is what I will go with. It is short and to the point, yet I believe it to be very representative of my writing. It is inspired by a well-known fairy tale, an

---

12. Including one special prize for academic writings. Three unrelated special mentions have also been given out over the years.

13. The Encouragement Prize had been awarded five times previously, always for French-language manuscripts. *The Pleasure of Drowning* is the first English-language work to win either Prize.

14. That, and the RHSfCIBsMS – that one still has me chuckling in the shower. The stories are good too, though.

anecdote I was once told, and the fact that I myself have always liked and worn long hair.

Foundations

This is where you get to know something about the city of Luxembourg. The first English-language short story I conceived, though not the first I wrote down, it is inspired by the legend of Luxembourg's foundation (in its various iterations) and my own work as a tourist guide. And yes, I wrote myself into it.

Stories, or Nothing Ever Happens in a Bar

The first story I finished, and the first one I read in front of an audience. If you entertain literary ambitions, there are really only three things to do: read, write and get out there. The first two are obvious, the third should be as well, but it's where many people stumble. No one cares how great your story is if it stays at home in your drawer. You have to confront yourself with the reader. A great way to start doing that is with readings in literary cafes, especially where discussion with the audience is encouraged. In Luxembourg, I would recommend two series of readings: Désœuvrés in the city, and Word in Progress in Esch. You have to be able to deal with feedback, though. Getting fifteen different reactions from twelve people is actually great – take what is useful to you and forget the rest.

This story's ending entails four different interpretations, three if you get rid of the usual cop-out: wine, blood, or the blood that is wine. You're welcome to come up with your own, though.

Cinderella in the Shoe
The Princess and the F***

Two more fairy tales. Two more stories.

Postcontemporary Beauty

My first story in a more science fiction or, at least, futuristic setting. I submitted it for a competition I was sure it would win. It didn't. You should submit your stories wherever you would like to see them appear. There's no downside to trying. You either win or … nothing. You can't lose something you didn't have before. Expect to be rejected – it's simple statistics – and keep trying until you aren't. Then start all over again. Just don't pay reading fees. You're already pouring your time, effort and soul into your work. That's enough.

This particular story is perhaps the most critical of the collection, bringing to the fore issues like gender-based violence and heteronormativity. These are central themes in a majority of the stories, which has a lot to do with the source material. However, depiction is not endorsement. The best a writer can hope for is to stumble onto some of the right questions.

Bluebeard

I hated Bluebeard as a child. Hated it. More than any story I'd ever come across. It just seemed so cruel and unnecessary. Had you told me then that I would one day write my own version of it ...

The Beauty of the Beast

The big one. If you're going to judge me on just one story, judge me on this one. Of course I'd rather you read all the stories ...

The Storyteller

What's that? That story doesn't appear in the collection? Well, it does now. This one was written for the first con I was a part of (Luxcon 2017), and I will dedicate it to Peadar Ó Guílin, whom I met there and whom I'll always be grateful to for introducing me to Ireland, Worldcon and Eurocon,[15] and, even more importantly, being a friend ...[16]

---

15. And here's the last piece of advice I am glad I was given: go to cons. If genre is your thing, this is where you meet people. Start with your local one if you're lucky enough to have one and, if you get a chance to attend Worldcon, kill anyone who stands in your way and attend.

16. If you want to know what Irish fairies are really like, read The Call – and never know another night of peaceful slumber.

There is magic in words, and even greater magic in names. He knew all the words and all the names. *His* name was his alone, and so people simply referred to him as the storyteller – if they referred to him at all. Mostly they didn't.

There was something eerie about the man, something unsettling. He was an outsider, of course, like all of his craft, a stranger by choice and by calling, but his was a very peculiar kind of strangeness. You would have ignored him, like you ignore all that don't belong, but he was impossible to ignore, just as he was impossible to make sense of. Uneasiness was his trademark.

You would have expected him to consort with fairies, but you would have been wrong. Fairies shunned him just like humans did.

He was a guardian of the old world, his function to remember. He was a wordsmith and a liar, his function to remind. He was a salesman of illusions and a maker of mirrors. He was man, he was god, he was nothing, he was all. He was a being of immense power, fragile as the fog. But he was a failure, and he was a fraud.

The Word was out of balance, the world as bad as new.

His was a painful path, full of rewards. He was sick at heart and sore of soul, his tongue as fresh as song. His joy was maddening and his sorrow dry. He knew what he had to do.

They came from all the corners and from all the circles. They came from the mountains and they came from the sea. They came from the skies and they came from the earth. They came from the forests and they came out of fire. They were tiny and enormous, colourful and pale, inconspicuous and incomprehensible, they were laughable, and they were death.

They all bowed to him.

He talked to them. He called them by their names. He drew them from the shadows and he made them whole again. He used every trick he had learned, every turn of phrase. He saved the Word. They … lived. They looked around and they acknowledged one another. He reminded them, and they remembered. Then, they ate the storyteller.

There. I'm about ready to make my exit. All that remains for me to say is that I wish you a pleasurable drowning, and hope it won't cause you any lasting harm. Oh, and one more thing: hello …

ACKNOWLEDGEMENTS

This is where I tell you that art isn't created in a vacuum and blah blah blah ... It's perfectly true, but if you are the kind of person who reads acknowledgements, you've already been told a hundred times.

So without further ado, I would like to acknowledge (and possibly thank) the following groups, individuals and entities:

My parents, for being there even when I don't want them to be.

My brother and my three sisters, for regularly refraining from strangling me.

Whoever wrote that book about the rabbit, for teaching me to read.

A mandarin and a duck, for teaching me to stand and to walk, respectively.

The writers and storytellers of my childhood, for allowing me to escape, and thus survive.

My cousin Gwenaël, for inspiring me to start writing my own stories.

My fifth and sixth-grade teacher Mr. Adams, for being my first adult reader and pretending my half-page of introduction to an epic centred on the duel between Michael and Lucifer at the end of times was actually interesting.

The city of Luxembourg, for saving my life.

William Shakespeare, for teaching me English (a few teachers helped as well).

My friends in high school and at university, for reconciliating me and keeping me in touch with the human species.

My friend Thierry, for giving me an excuse to start writing again.

David Benioff and D. B. Weiss, for introducing me to George R. R. Martin.

George R. R. Martin, for having me read fantasy again.

The 2013 edition of the Concours Littéraire National, for giving me an excuse to start writing again, and its jury, for rewarding my efforts.

Neil Gaiman, for having me write fantasy again and having me write it in English and in the form of short stories.

The Luxembourg City Tourist Office, for the privilege of being a tour guide in the most beautiful city in the world (all right, so I might not be entirely impartial).

Ian De Toffoli, for being my first impresario.

Isabelle Junck and Jeff Schinker at Désœuvrés and Nathalie Ronvaux, Claire Leydenbach (she of the perfect name) and Jeff Schinker (again) at Word in Progress.

Luc Caregari, Jill Christophe, Sandy Artuso and the team at ILL, for giving me my first paid job as a writer.

Gérard Kraus and the team behind the SFFS Luxembourg and Luxcon, for introducing me to the world of conventions and Peadar Ó Guilín.

Peadar, for introducing me to Ireland and being my friend.

The writers at Luxcon and in particular the excellent crop of 2019 featuring Aliette de Bodard, Adrian Tchaikovsky, Elizabeth Bear, Scott Lynch and the inescapable Peadar Ó Guilín, for making me see the world I want to live in.

Jeanne Glesener and the jury of the Prix Servais 2019, for awarding me the Prix d'Encouragement, Germaine Goetzinger and the team of the Servais Foundation, as well as Claude Conter and the team of the CNL, for making it all possible, Valerija Berdi and Nathalie Bender from Radio 100,7, for being the best of laudators and interviewers, respectively, and Elise Schmit, for being the best person imaginable to receive a literary award with.

Peadar, for introducing me to Worldcon and Eurocon.

The people at and behind Worldcon and Eurocon, for being amazing.

The team of Luna Press Publishing, led by the Luna

Space Beagle with the assistance of the amazing Francesca T. Barbini and Robert S. Malan, for making dreams come true.

Carolina Cancanilla, for a better cover than I could have hoped or dreamed.

Peadar Ó Guilín (Will you stop haunting these acknowledgements already?) and Sam J. Miller, for playing the game and dragging my name through the mud, and Nico Helminger, who was just trying to pay me an actual compliment.

The people who deserve to be mentioned, but weren't, either because I ran out of gas (That's a terrible analogy; since when am I a car?), because I am not cognizant of or willing to admit their merits, or because I simply forgot (which I will most certainly deny).

You, for reading through the acknowledgements section.[1]

---

1. Who does that, anyway? All right, *I* do, but I'm crazy. What's your excuse?

www.ingramcontent.com/pod-product-compliance
Lightning Source LLC
Chambersburg PA
CBHW030647190726
48286CB00008B/2698